For Mike,
In print ♡
last after all
years ... briefly.
Dave

Great Writers Indecently Exposed

LITERATURE
IN
BRIEFS

Edited by William Zaranka
Illustrated by Dave Werner

Apple-wood Books
Cambridge/Watertown

Grateful acknowledgment is made for permission to reprint the following:

Jedidiah Barrow: From *The New Statesman*, 1973. Reprinted by permission of The Statesman & Nation Publishing Co. Ltd.

Gerard Benson: From *The New Statesman*, March 22, 1974. Reprinted by permission of The Statesman & Nation Publishing Co. Ltd.

John Dennis: From *The New Statesman*, February 15, 1974. Reprinted by permission of The Statesman & Nation Publishing Co.Ltd

Corey Ford: From *The John Riddell Murder Case*, Copyright + 1930, 1957 by Corey Ford. Reprinted by permission of Harold Ober Associates Incorpated.

Robert Goldman, From *National Lampoon's*, *This Side of Parodies*, Warner Paperback Library, first printing February, 1974. + 1970 National Lampoon, Inc. Reprinted by permission of *National Lampoon*.

Henry Hetherington, From *The New Statesman*, December 19,1975. Reprinted by permisson of The Statesman & Nation Publishing Co. Ltd.

Tim Hopkins: From *The New Statesman*, December 19, 1975. Reprinted by permission of The Statesman & Nation Publishing Co. Ltd.

Leslie Johnson: From *The New Statesman*, July 7, 1951. Reprinted by permission of The Statesman & Nation Publishing Co. Ltd.

Russel Lucas: From *The New Statesman, November 22, 1974. Reprinted by permission of The Statesman Publishing Co. Ltd.*

Mary Ann Madden: From Maybe He's Dead. Reprinted by permission of the author.

M.J. Monk: From *The New Statesman*, October 2, 1970. Reprinted by permission of The Statesman & Nation Publishing Co. Ltd.

E.O. Parrott: From *The New Statesman*, May 27, 1977. Reprinted by permission of The Statesman & Publishing Co. Ltd.

Andrea Paterson: Reprinted by permission of the author.

A.L. Thon: From *The New Statesman*, September 14, 1964. Reprinted by permission of The Statesman & Nation Publishing Co. Ltd.

David Watkin: From *The New Statesman*, April 25, 1975. Reprinted by permission of The Statesman & Nation Publishing Co. Ltd.

Craig Weeden: First appeared in *Poultry*, Vol. 1, 1. Reprinted by permission of the author.

William Zaranka: Appeared originally in *Antigonish Review*. Reprinted with their permission and the permission of the author.

ISBN: 0-918222-58-3

AL 1 2 3 4 5 6 7 8 9 0

LITERATURE
IN
BRIEFS

For Suzanne
—D.W.
To My Wife, Ruth
—W.Z.

CONTENTS

Chaucer's *The Probatioun Officeres Tale* 13

Shakespeare's *Soliloquy* 15

Austen's From *Unpleasantness at the*
OK Corral 17

Longfellow's *Hiawatha Revisited* 19

Poe's *Seasonal Rentals:*
The House of Usher 21

Whitman's *Jack and Jill* 23

Dickinson's *Because I Could Not Dump* 27

Anderson's *Discord: A Story* 29

Frost's *Left-Leaning TRESPASSERS WILL*
BE SHOT Sign 31

Wodehouse's From *Bertie and Emma* 37

Lawrence's From *Peanuts* 39

Pound's *You Call That a Ts'ing: A Letter* 41

Tolkien's From *The Spirit Of*
Middle Earth 43

Hemingway's *Jack Sprat* 45

Salinger's From *The Grand Old*
Duke of York 47

Ginsberg's *A Pizza Joint in Cranston* 49

Fleming's From *Dr. Nope* 53

Spillane's From *The Nun Runner* 55
Krantz's *My First Day at School* 57
Plath's *Ragout* 59
Segal's *Sob Story* 61

A Parody by Gerard Benson

GEOFFREY CHAUCER's
The Probatioun Officeres Tale

The lede guiterriste was a craftie ladde,
Wel koude he luren chickes to his padde
To dyg the sownes of Clapton or The Stones
And share a joynte and turn on for the nones,
Till met he with a drogge squadde maiden fayre
Who yaf him think she was a Frenssche au pair,
That whan at last he caused hir sens to feynte
And subtilly to frote hir at the queynte,
And whyspere sucred words and strook her sore,
"Lay on!" she cried, "my rammysh prikasour!"
For she was nothing loth to amorous sport
So be she got hir Pusheres into court.

A Parody by T.F. Dillon Croker

WILLIAM SHAKESPEARE's
Soliloquy

To shave, or not to shave? that is the question,
Whether 'tis comfortable most to cover
One's face all over with outrageous lather,
Or by outrageous hair, s(h)ave so much trouble,
And thus soap-pose we end it! To shave — to swear
What for? when by moustache and beard we end
The nuisance thus encouraging the locks
That flesh is *hair* to — 'tis a consummation
Devoutly to be wished. To shave? To swear?
To swear! perchance an oath — ay, there's the rub;
For as we shave, perhaps the razor slips,
And as we *barber*ously hack our chin,
Must we then pause; in every respect
There is calamity in such a shave.

A Parody by David Watkin

JANE AUSTEN's
From *Unpleasantness at the OK Corral*

The next morning was fair, and Earp almost expected another attack from the assembled posse. With Dr. Halliday to support him he felt no dread of the event: but he would gladly be spared a shootout, where victory itself was painful; and was heartily rejoiced therefore at neither seeing nor hearing anything of them.

The Clantons arrived at the appointed time; and no new difficulty arising, no sudden recollection, no unexpected summons, no impertinent intrusion to disconcert their measure, our heroes were most unnaturally able to fulfil their engagement. They determined on walking round the OK Corral, that ignoble enclosure, whose isolated position renders it so striking an object from almost every opening in Tombstone.

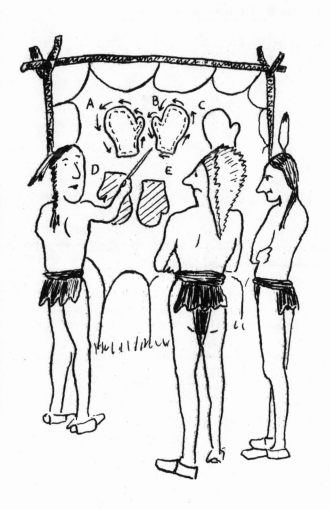

A Parody by George A. Strong

HENRY WADSWORTH LONGFELLOW'S
Hiawatha Revisited

When he killed the Mudjokivis,
Of the skin he made him mittens,
Made them with the fur side inside,
Made them with the skin side outside,
He, to get the warm side inside,
Put the inside skin side outside;
He, to get the cold side outside,
Put the warm side fur side inside,
That's why he put the fur side inside.
Why he put the skin side outside,
Why he turned them inside outside.

A Parody by Leslie Johnson

EDGAR ALLAN POE's
Seasonal Rentals: The House of Usher

Sole surviving male representative of well-known ancient family, much attached to his old Gothic mansion (well off beaten track, with most distinctive atmosphere, a veritable voice from the dead past) is prepared to receive a few paying guests of the right sort before the fall. Special treatment for nervous disorders; family physician constantly in attendance. No jollifications. Commodious, lofty, airy rooms. Lake (not suitable for bathing). Recherche cuisine. Own fungi grown on premises in great profusion and variety. Unique cellar. Those who genuinely wish to bury themselves in the country should apply to R. Usher, House of Usher.

A Parody by Charles Battell Loomis

WALT WHITMAN's
Jack and Jill

I celebrate the personality of Jack!
I love his dirty hands, his tangled hair, his
   locomotion blundering.
Each wart upon his hands I sing,
Paeans I chant to his hulking shoulder blades.
Also Jill!
Her I celebrate.
I, Walt, of unbridled thought and tongue,
Whoop her up!
Her golden hair, her sun-struck face, her hard and
   reddened hands;
So, too, her feet, hefty, shambling.
I see them in the evening, when the sun empurples
   the horizon, and through the darkening forest
   aisles are heard the sounds of myriad creatures of
   the night.
I see them climb the steep ascent in quest of
   water for their mother.
Oh, speaking of her, I could celebrate the old
   lady if I had time.
She is simply immense!

But Jack and Jill are walking up the hill.
(I didn't mean that rhyme.)
I must watch them.
I love to watch their walk,
And wonder as I watch;

He, stoop-shouldered, clumsy, hide-bound,
Yet lusty,
Bearing his share of the 1-lb bucket as though it
    were a paperweight.
She, erect, standing, her head uplifting,
Holding, but bearing not the bucket.
They have reached the spring.
They have filled the bucket.
Have you heard the "Old Oaken Bucket"?
I will sing it: —

Of what countless patches is the bed-quilt of life
    composed!
Here is a piece of lace. A babe is born.
The father is happy, the mother is happy.
Next black crepe. A beldame "shuffles off this
    mortal coil."
Now brocaded satin with orange blossoms.
Mendelssohn's "Wedding March," an old shoe
    missile,
A broken carriage window, the bride in the
    Bellevue sleeping.
Here's a large piece of black cloth!
"Have you any last words to say?"
"No."
"Sheriff, do your work!"

Thus it is: from "grave to gay, from lively to
    severe."

I mourn the downfall of my Jack and Jill
I see them descending, obstacles not heeding.
I seem them pitching headlong, the water from the
    pail outpouring, a noise from leathern lungs
    out-belching.

The shadows of the night descend on Jack,
    recumbent, bellowing, his pate with gore
    besmeared.
I love his cowardice, because it is an attribute,
    just like
Job's patience or Solomon's wisdom, and I love
    attributes.
Whoop!!!

A Parody by Andrea Paterson

EMILY DICKINSON's
Because I Could Not Dump

Because I could not Dump the Trash —
Joe kindly stopped for Me —
The Garbage Truck held but Ourselves —
And Bacterial Colonies —

We slowly drove — Joe smelled of Skunk —
Yet risking no delay
My hairdo and composure too,
Were quickly Fumed away —

We passed a School, where Dumpsters stood
Recycling — in the Rain —
We picked up Yields of Industry —
Dead Cats and Window Panes —

Or rather — Joe picked up —
Seeing maggot-lined cans — I recoiled —
When heir to smelly Legacies,
What sort of Woman — Spoils?

We paused before a Dump that seemed
A Swelling of the Ground —
The soil was scarcely visible —
Joe dropped — his Booty — down.

Since then — 'tis a fortnight — yet
Seems shorter than the Day
I first set out the Old Fish Heads —
And hoped Joe'd come my Way —

A Parody by Corey Ford

SHERWOOD ANDERSON's
Discord: A Story

It was dark. He was coming home alone. The man was coming home alone.

He came to the door of his home, 67 South Hickory Street, and he took out his key. Such a time. He could not find the lock. That is, he could not find *which* lock. There were between one hundred and seventy-five and two hundred locks on the door. You know how it was. Besides, he had the wrong key anyway.

He knocked at the door.

He said: "Oh, Ethel dear."

His wife, Mrs. Stoops, opened the door. "Llewellyn!"

Years of bitterness welled up within her. Years of struggle. Years of pain. No, tears of pain. Tears of pain and bitterness. Why had he stayed so late? Where had he been? "Where have you been?" "Nowheres, m'dear." "Oh, yeah?"

Years of desertion. That time he was playing the swell blonde, for example. Sometimes he didn't come home for a week at a time. Said he was working at the office. "I've been working late at the office, dear, and I won't get home to-night." Sure, sure. A likely story. She thought of that, too.

"Let me in, dearest."

He had been drinking. She could smell his breath. Suddenly she hated him. Her fist swings out. She hits him.

Then they go inside.

God knows, God knows.

29

A Parody by William Zaranka

ROBERT FROST's
Left-Leaning TRESPASSERS WILL BE SHOT Sign

I stood and watched him dig one hole all day.
He finally got it deep enough to sink
A post of rotten oak, then wedge it in
With rocks he chose out of the pile he'd made.
He'd need ten years of digging for one fence
With that small spade he used, all bent and
    splined
Like a fork a tractor mowed.
            "Friend," I said,
"I own a post-hole digger. Own it clear.
And you can buy one cheap at Murphy's store."

He nodded and he looked me in the eye,
The kind of proud-flesh nod or wince or shrug
A horse makes when it's lashed across the snout,
Then started counting off the steps between
My property and his, where with his rotten posts
He'd fence us off. Then he came back and winked,
The kind of desperate wink a hired man winks
When asked to read a letter he can't read:

"Last thing I need's a post-hole digger, friend."

"The soil is stingy here, it will not yield,"
I said, "except to men with sense enough
To use the proper tool to make it yield.
You aim to dig a fence, you need to use

The proper tool. If anything, it's that
Which separates us from the savages,
The way we men with bigger brains use tools
To dig our holes and save our fingernails."

He puzzled and he sniffed his fingernails.
"You got a point. I need an oil rig."

I held a chuckle down. "But why an oil rig?"
"Well, I don't know. Except it smells like oil.
It feels like oil. Bet you it even burns."

He was so poor, so threadbare hopeful poor,
This man smelling his thumbs on my front porch,
He thought that all he had to do was dig
One hole and out gushed oil, or plant one seed
And up an apple or a cherry orchard sprang.
"You say that you struck oil?" I challenged him.

"The map I got says oil. The well's supposed
To run just my side of the boundary line.
Just lookit how them swallows veer away
From it. Them swallows know there ain't no bugs
To catch and eat on oil-bearin' land."

"It's hard to tell which way a swallow veers.
That's motor-oil," I challenged him again.

"Well, I don't own no tractor nor no truck,"
He snapped, and turned his heel, and walked away.

I called to him: "You say you've got a map?"

He grinned and shrugged: "Well, I ain't sayin',"
   he said.
You know how digging holes all night can be.
Something there is that makes you want to quit,
To take your post-hole-digger and go home
And light a candle. Birds are all asleep,
Except the owl who flashes, talons first,
Out of the nightmare dark to pince a mouse,
And shred it back upon his branch again.
Accomplishing one hole, and then the next,
And then the next: why, that's the only thing
That keeps you going almost until dawn,
Except if it's a newborn sense of pride
In helping a new neighbor who needs help,
But who's too proud to ask you for some help.

At noon I heard a knock.
       "Come take a look,"
He said, pointing at the post-holes I had dug.
"Somebody tried to steal my oil last night."

There are some men who'd rather point a thief
Than admit a charity in their behalf.
And so I let him have his little wrath.
The poor illusion of his need was what
He needed most. I didn't say a word.

"They must of dug all night, and whatya think?
That map's a fluke. There ain't one drop of oil
I guess I'll put me up a little fence."

He sunk his posts. He strung two barbed-wire lines

Between his shingle-blasted house and mine.
The last thing that he did that day was nail
A sign onto the post of rotten oak:
TRESPASSERS WILL BE SHOT ON SIGHT, it read.

There are no cattle here. None to keep off.
That barbed wire is the spirit of the man
Strung out and gleaming like a set of teeth.
At night it sings like bow-string in the wind.

I call to him each day,
            "That sign of yours,
It leans a little too much to the left,
onto my property."
            And he agrees,
But not to make it right, or take it down.

A Parody by Russell Lucas

P.G. WODEHOUSE's
From Bertie and Emma

"I'm so unhappy," Emma Bovary sighed, as she rested her head on Bertie's shoulder. "I say, cheer up old thing," he exhorted, patting her back with imprudent familiarity. He quivered as her warm flesh seared his trembling body. She raised her mouth towards his and Bertie snorted with undisguised passion. "I'm not terribly good at this sort of rot," he confided, before clamping his lips against her. "Take me dearest," she moaned helplessly. His knees buckled with excitement and he slithered to the carpet with Emma. Bertie closed his eyes discreetly as he glimpsed her bared shoulders, yet held on with the resolution of an unmitigated bounder. "Now," she insisted urgently. Bertie was engulfed by panic. "Would you mind dreadfully if I phoned Jeeves?" he bleated.

A Parody by John Dennis

D. H. LAWRENCE's
From *Peanuts*

The baseball mound!

And there stands Charlie Brown. A hotch-potch of yearnings for the little red-haired girl. But the game is a fulfillment. Baseball. The savage soul-conflict, gladiatorial, the *tlachti* of the Aztecs.

On his hand, a glove. One glove. It's an amputation. Why, even Wotan, giving up an eyeball, didn't make a sacrifice like that.

And Lucy, *She* lies in ecstasy against the piano, while Schneider batters away in an insanity of pure self-destruction. America. The piano is America and poor hopeless Schneider is trying to teach it Beethoven when all that will come is dissonances.

So Lucy sets up as a psychiatrist. The Doctor is In. She wants to forget Schneider and his queer mechanical outpourings. And all she gets is the poor sick soul of America, Charlie Brown, pining to be loved by the great cruel world.

A Parody by Jedediah Barrow

EZRA POUND's
You Call That a Ts'ing: A Letter

When I was a girl I sat with the old men.
Or watching my cherry blossom
I would play with your ts'ing.*
When the birds flew westward
I came to the Province of So Ho
Where no cherry is to be found.
But the old men turned up.
They rose like carp to the feeding hand.
Now after too many months I sit alone.
I mark the days on my calendar.
When you read these words
Clasp your ts'ing and come.

*An instrument similar to a d'ong but smaller. (trans.)

A Parody by E. O. Parrott

J.R.R. TOLKIEN's
From *The Spirit of Middle Earth*

Smirnoff was known as Smirrm's Knoff to the Red
Dwarves of Voll-Gah, which lies far to the east of Eridor,
where Smirrm, a fiery dragon over two miles long,
dwelt beside Allko-Holl, the Liquid Mountain. It is said
that the dragon made this delicious-tasting spirit from
herbs gathered by the Elven folk in Elrond on the night of
the first full moon after Mirkwyre Day. The Hobbits tell
how the Goblins lusted after the recipe of the Knoff, and
many times tried in vain to steal it, but it was lost after
Smirrm was slain by Starlyn, a wandering Orc. After
many moons the precious parchment came, no one
knows how, into the hands of Andsorr the Bibulous,
who gave it to Gandalf. Gandalf managed to decipher
Smirrm's runes, and made the wonderful drink himself,
and guarded its secret with more care that he gave to the
Great Ring itself. But because he is wise, Gandalf has
now made it available to the Men of the West. As
Gandalf said: "I could not tell an Orc from an old
Andsorr until I rediscovered Smirrm's Knoff."

Smirnoff — the very spirit of Middle Earth.

A Parody by Henry Hetherington

ERNEST HEMINGWAY's
Jack Sprat

"Come in, Jack."

"I d'wanta come in."

"D'wanta come in, hell. Come in bright boy."

They went in.

"I'll have eats now," she said. She was fat and red.

"I'd want nothing," Jack said. He was thin and pale.

"D'want nothin' hell. You have eats now, bright boy."

She called the waiter. "Bud," she said, "gimme bacon and beans — twice."

Bud brought the bacon and beans.

"I d'want bacon. It's too fat," Jack said.

"D'want bacon, hell. I'll eat the fat. You eat the lean. OK big boy?"

"OK," Jack said.

They had eats.

"Now lick the plate clean," she said.

"Aw, honey," said Jack, "I ain't gotta, do I?"

"Yup," she said. "You gotta."

They both licked their plates clean.

A Parody by Tim Hopkins

J. D. SALINGER's
The Grand Old Duke Of York

There was this goddam English duke for Chrissake —
and boy wasn't he just so damn grand and all. Anyway,
this crazy sonuvabitch has this bunch of ten thousand
crumby West Point rejects who are about as much use to
him as a hole in the head. So this crazy duke walks the
ass off these jerks up and down this lousy goddam hill.
And these GIs work it out that when they reach the top of
this hill they're up for Chrissake and when they reach
the bottom they're down for Chrissake — which is a
pretty big deal. Anyway there's this real smart sonuvabitch and he blew everyone's goddam mind when he
says that halfway up is not up and not down neither. But
you know — I felt kinda sorry for the guy. I get like that
sometimes — and when he spoke, I was damn near
bawling. I really was.

A Parody by Craig Weeden

ALLEN GINSBERG's
A Pizza Joint in Cranston

What thoughts I have of you tonight, Walt
    Whitman, for I work late at Ernie's Pizza and Grinders
    with a headache self-conscious looking at the bulge
    under my apron.

In my hungry fatigue, and cooking for images, I've
    been fondling tomatoes, dreaming of your recipes!
What sauce and combinations! Whole families eating
    together! Mouths oozing pizza! Wives gorging
    mushrooms! Babies stuck under mozzarella! — and
    you Garcia Lorca, What do you mean it needs more
    oregano?
I saw you, Walt Whitman, childless, lonely old
    grubber, poking among the olives and eyeing the sub
    rolls.
I saw you sneaking samples of each: Who pays I
    ask? You smile, salami in your beard.

I wander in and out of bins of chopped onions and
    anchovies following you, and followed in my
    imagination by Ernie himself.
We strode down by heaps of dough in our solitary
    fancy tasting my special dressing, possessing the key
    to the coke machine, and never passing the cashier.

Where are we going, Walt Whitman? The oven shuts
   down in an hour. Where will the salami drop off your
   beard tonight?
(I touch your book and dream of oddyssey in the
   men's room and feel absurd.)
Will we walk all night through the solitary
   streets? The trees add shade to shade, lights out in the
   houses, we'll both be lonely and burp pizza.
Will we stroll dreaming of super combinations of
   the ultimate sandwich, home to our silent cottage?

Ah dear father, crudbeard, lonely old cooking
   teacher, what bicarbonate did you have when Ernie
   quit poling his ferry and started this franchise leaving
   you with stomach cramps on the black streets of
   Cranston?

A Parody by A.L. Thom

IAN FLEMING'S
Dr. Nope

As the sinister purple light winked again, the enormous eunuchs dragged Bond towards the massive steel door.

"In there, Bond," said the unseen whisperer, "are creatures much more formidable than any you have ever encountered. I observe that you are quivering — with curiosity."

The door opened silently.

"Take him in!" commanded the whisperer. "Release him — carefully. He is a little — fatigued."

Bond darted a swift glance round the luxuriously furnished chamber.

"Yes, Bond," said the whisperer. "Women. Twenty beautiful women. All nymphomaniacs. None has enjoyed a man for months. Some are naked, some dressed, some in deshabille, some clad as boys. Doubtless you will have your preference."

A naked half-caste woman stood before Bond. From her sleek black hair to her scarlet toenails, she was perfect. In a sudden frenzy of lust she threw herself upon him, kissing, biting, clawing, sobbing. Bond seized her by the throat. His only hope was to strangle, say, 15 of them. But many soft, urgent, experienced hands were caressing susceptible parts of his body, and soon he fell to the floor, writhing helplessly.

A Parody by M.J. Monk

MICKEY SPILLANE'S
From *The Nun Runner*

"C'mon baby," I said, "you'll just have to kick the habit."

"Keeka de habit? No understan'."

"You can do better than that, sweetheart," I said. "Shed the wrappers, show the goods, peel!"

She still played dumb. But she wasn't fooling me. She wasn't fooling anyone anymore. Not now.

"Okay, baby, if that's how you want to play it." I tore off the starched white headgear and the familiar platinum blond hair cascaded on to her shoulders. There was fear in her eyes now. She tried to run but I got my fingers in the back of her robe. There was a harsh tearing noise and she spun round, backed up against the door with a pile of black cotton round her ankles. She was still wearing the same gold star transfers. In all the right places.

"Let's go, sister," I said.

A Parody by Mary Ann Madden

JUDITH KRANTZ's
My First Day at School

April Rane shuddered into the clinging Pucci and turned to appraise herself in the full length mirror. "Perfect," she thought, "the body of a twenty-year old." She held the large gold hoops to her ears. "Too much," she decided. No sense diverting attention from the sleek chestnut hair caressing her shoulders. Once more she twirled before the mirror — a flick of mascara — and smiled at her reflection. April tiptoed across the bedroom (Brick was still asleep), picked up her pencil box, and with a soft click the door closed upon summer. "P.S. 501 look out," she breathed, "here comes April Rane."

A Parody by William Zaranka

SYLVIA PLATH's
Ragout

What a trick —
Your prick instead of a carrot.
O pinch of pepper lover,
My soprano man,

Once a week I try it, I do,
Whetting the carving knives,
Making a stew,
A stew of the privates of you.

Dashed with paprika, it's you.
Blue on the butcher-block, you
A less Fascist, tenderized you.

Come into my ticklish kitchen!
Where the toil is,
Where the tinfoil is,
And the balls are ground live
In the blender.

Ich, ich, ich, yum, yum, yum:
A ragout.
And it tastes like nobody but you.

A Parody by Robert Goldman

ERIC SEGAL'S
Sob Story

Chapter 16

It's not all that easy to make a best seller.

Ask Ernie Hemingway (a Princeton man). Ernie Hemingway never made the top of the *New York Times* Best Seller List. Ernie Hemingway could take a lesson from Mrs. Naomi Greenbaum Oliver Bartlett XV.

We were sitting down over dinner. We had bought great Jap sterling steel silverware.

"If they want to laugh," she said, "they watch Red Skelton. If they're gonna shell out four ninety-five for a slim book with short sentences, you gotta give them something to cry about."

I shoveled another forkful of cocktail onions into my mouth and masticated thoughtfully. Sure enough, the tears started coming. Before I knew it, I was bawling like a baby.

"Don't just sit there, Preppie," Naomi yelled, "get to that typewriter!"

I did just that. Two hours and three hundred cocktail onions later, I had finished the first twelve chapters.

Chapter 17

Naomi took a job in a cannery while I tried to finish the novel. I say tried because after a hundred pages, I still didn't have the grabber. I scoured back issues of *Modern Romance* until my fingers were stained with ink and the pulp was soggy with tears. Still, I didn't find the plot twist I needed. Then, one night, the answer came to me.

Naomi had come home from work and I decided to have some fun with her.

"Thought you were packing sardines," I said.

"Preppie, I am," she replied. "Who told you different?"

"My nose," I said. "It tells me you're packing smelts!"

Naomi laughed. Then she collapsed.

"Love is all you need," she gasped. "But just to make sure, get a big advance."